S.

Of

Mayhem, Murder, & Romance

Catherine Grace

JP

This paperback edition published 2020 by Jasami Publishing Ltd
an imprint of Jasami Publishing Ltd
Glasgow, Scotland
https://jasamipublishingltd.com

ISBN 978-1-913798-11-6

Acknowledgements

I must acknowledge the professor who long ago said I should publish my stories, and friends throughout the years who have encouraged this idea and enjoyed my little writings. Most notably Russell, Paula, Lesley, and Ian who have all been active participants in supporting me throughout this process.

Dedication

This book is dedicated to my Mum and Dad
I miss you both every day.

Contents

Lost

Language is a thing of beauty…the meaning of a word can express so much in so many different ways - for instance, the word Lost.

I've lost ten pounds - great celebration!

I got lost today - begs the question physically, mentally, or emotionally.

I've lost my gloves, an umbrella, a book, my job - all things that can be replaced.

I've lost my parents, my sister, my brother, my child - all loved ones are irreplaceable.

I've lost my way - again physical, mental, or emotional?

Some items are not really lost - they are either hiding or just not with us at the moment

We can always find gloves or a job, and we never go looking to replace the ten pounds we lost…

So don't spend time looking for something that may not return - just embrace and accept and deal with the new!

I make this observation only because I have no idea how to find the 2" I lost - going from 5'7" to 5'5" - and if you happen to find them somewhere no worries - I'm happy!

I kinda like being a bit shorter :)…

and by the way…when someone says get lost - lose them and go have an Adventure!

Or maybe for just a little while - you will get Lost in these stories.

The BBQ

Cassandra surveyed the dead body at her feet. "This is definitely a problem," she thought, "no one will believe it was an accident."

While the first shot might have been, the following four were decidedly not. She viewed the face that now reflected none of the cruelty he had subjected her to, and nudged the muscular arm that had left so many bruises to ensure her husband was truly and unquestionably dead then proceeded to consider her options. Calling the police was out of the question, they would tote her off to jail in a heartbeat, and yet not calling them presented the issue of explaining his absence.

Cassandra turned and, strolling into the kitchen, stopped at the dilapidated fridge to pull out a bottle of white wine. She poured a large glass and, as she sipped it, an idea, which she rejected at first began to formulate in her mind; she reconsidered and finally decided to go ahead with it.

Fifteen minutes later through sheer will, her diminutive figure dragged his body to the area where he usually dressed his illegal kills of venison and other meats, it was perfect since it was already covered in a bloody mess and she smiled at the irony.

"Cassie this pork is delicious" raved Lucinda at the BBQ the following day.

"Yep." Agreed Harry, helping himself to another huge portion of the delectable meat.

"I only cooked it. Richard provided the meat himself." Cassandra replied, trying not to wince at the abbreviated use of her name while at the same time inwardly smiling at his meat provision.

"Unusual he's missing his own party. Where is he by the way?" Asked John as he helped himself to another of the pork burgers.

Cassandra had considered this carefully all night, and so replied. "It couldn't be helped, Sonora County police showed up and said he had to briefly appear in court today, but I know he'll be back soon, they never do keep him very long." She sighed holding her breath as she waited for the reactions.

Harry sniggered as the meaty juice ran down his chubby stubbled chin, and as usual, he let the dirty hanky tucked into his shirt soak up the mess.

"Can't believe he'd let you host this yourself." He stated winking at her, the smile showing black and jagged teeth.

"As I said, he'll be here soon enough. As a matter of fact, I feel he is already here in spirit." Cassandra replied in a light tone and continued, "would you like another beer, Harry?"

"Don't mind if I do."

Cassandra immediately headed to the beer cooler.

"Whatcha smiling at?" Erica asked, suddenly appearing at her elbow.

"Just thinking how much Richard loves this annual BBQ." Cassandra answered, proud she remembered to use the present tense.

Her phone buzzed and as she turned to answer it she raised her voice. "Hi honey."

She kept the one-way conversation short ending with, "I'll leave right now to pick you up, sweetie."

A few minutes later Cassandra was just opening the door of her car when Harry sauntered up. "Wait a sec! I just found this in my pork burger."

She turned and suddenly felt nauseous as she saw Richard's golden wedding ring glistening in Harry's plumb palm.

"Guess it must have fallen off when he dressed the pig. Now you make sure he gets it back," he dictated.

Harry dropped the greasy glistening golden ring into Cassandra's outstretched hand.

She gave a feeble smile as her hand folded around the ring and answered, "thanks Harry, I surely will. See ya soon."

She slipped behind the wheel of her red convertible happy knowing that this was absolutely the last time she would see any of them and sped off, adding the value of that gold ring to the stash of jewellery that would make her new start a most comfortable one.

The Lady Jane

The last few rays of warm sun receded behind the hill bidding the choppy seas a colourful farewell. How she would miss moments like this, the golden sun, the black sea, the craggy, dangerous shore. Fifty years ago, *The Lady Jane* embarked upon the sea and since then had fulfilled every one of her master's commands, from fishing to storing precious cargo and all the while bringing the crew safely back home.

The predicted storm was blowing in but as she felt the squall begin to rise there was something more ominous behind the black and violently crashing waves. Then suddenly the inky sky merged with the blackened stormy sea creating complete darkness that was only shattered by the frothy white of breaking water as it gushed over her.

The sounds of the storm receded for only a moment when she heard the angry voices and the pathetic plaintiff cry engulfed in a strangled death, and in that instant she knew her master was gone.

Soon afterward she felt the creepy skulking movements of those who had murdered her master, those scheming brutal pirates who were after the secret, who were after the treasure.

Throughout the years the master had protected *The Lady Jane* and made sure she was safeguarded, sheltered, and cared for; and she had done the same for him. Now, she knew that she would reciprocate, those who had violated her master would pay the price!

What to do? What to do? The secret treasure must be protected at all cost! And she would do it! The storm was her protection. The seaside harbour had always been her haven yet it now would become her inevitable destination, there would be no sand to envelop her in safety only a jagged rocky death providing her a final resting place.

So she gave herself up to the stormy night to be buffeted, blown and crushed, and so quickly the waves drove her upon the banks of the shore and she endured the end laying upon her side still protecting her master and the treasure while casting his murderers upon the waves to be dragged into the depths of the sea.

As *The Lady Jane* lay upon the shore and the waters ebbed away she felt the loss of the water that had kept her on an even keel for fifty years, reflecting and wondering if this was how fish, who lay still tangled in a net after a long and weary fight? That did not matter, what mattered was she now knew her master and the treasure were safe.

The next morning the villagers saw *The Lady Jane* grounded damaged beyond restoration, and the Captain who had been her only master for fifty years was found in his cabin. People commented on the strangest part of the tragedy, the fact that the figurehead was undamaged except for a single tear which suddenly appear and had never been carved into the original. So, the mystery remains of *The Lady Jane*, her *Captain*, and the secret hidden in the depths of the enigmatic sea.

The Last Sandcastle

The sandcastle was taking good shape he thought when heard the whiney, "Dickie don't make that side so big," from the skinny pale girl. Rolling his eyes, he made the change. "Ooooh much better, now put another turret on the other side." Complying he made the correction with sadness in his heart knowing that he would miss his sister.

She and He

Glancing up from the page of her book she gently wriggled the red painted toes of her right foot, which succeeded in creating a small humpff and a hand pulling at her big toe, causing it to stiffen and then relax.

She reflected on the face before her and smiled, it was not handsome, not dashing, but warm and comfortable, full of tenderness and love. The chaise they reclined on was large enough to allow an expansive comfort so each could see the other while remaining wrapped pleasantly together.

He turned slightly and brushed his lips against the instep of her foot, and she felt a small tickle with a tingle of pleasure. His long lashes brushed his cheek which was so incongruous to his lack of hair which he jokingly referred to as his very high forehead, and as this was his only vanity for that she cared little.

She closed her eyes and remembered their first meeting so many years ago. Was it really over three decades? It seemed like a lifetime and yet in other ways it seemed as if it were only yesterday, and so she allowed the memory to flow in like a soft and gentle tide.

It was the tiny pub downstairs from the cramped flat she shared with two friends, and once a week they would all splurge their meagre student income on drinks with fish and chips.

They met when she was at the bar to request a fresh bottle of vinegar. At the same moment, they both reached for the bottle and their fingers touched for an electrifying moment.

"Excuse me," he apologised.

"Oh no I'm sorry," she replied

She looked up into his face, which reflected his kind and gentle nature, and she smiled. He returned her gaze and turning a faint pink he pushed the bottle toward her, releasing it.

"Please do."

"Thank you," and smiling again she noticed his eyes were the colour of a stormy sea dark with small specks of grey.

As he returned her gaze, he was immediately captivated by her sky-blue eyes set in a perfect heart-shaped face surrounded by waves of ebony hair.

He blushed more deeply.

"Thank you again," she said turning to weave her way through the crowded tables back to her friends clutching the much-desired bottle in hand.

"Now that you have won the battle for the vinegar, please do share," said her friends, holding out their hands, "We're starving!"

She remembered glancing back at the counter and he was gone. She didn't look around, she could not, just the same, his eyes, so much depth, so much emotion. For a brief moment she thought, *he was probably just being polite, but still, there was a connection.* She did not realise exactly how strong that connection would prove to be.

A soft exhale of breath brought her back to the present, she opened her eyes and was met with now so familiar eyes the colour of a stormy sea.

"Where art thou?"

"Remembering that first moment, when you so unashamedly tried to steal my vinegar bottle." She laughed.

"I protest, you tried to steal it first. I was merely being a gentleman." And his hand reached to tickle her foot, which she promptly pulled away and tucked under her leg.

"Oh, bother I was quite comfortable," she complained in a light and loving voice.

He blushed then gently requested, "return your foot and I do so promise to be the gentleman of your dreams."

She returned it, wiggling it once again into a comfortable place.

"You already are."

He squinted one eye, "I refuse to believe in such an early submission."

She blinked quickly preventing a tear. "Never! I just thought I would lull you into complacency. And in this content and lovely moment would you be inclined to pour the last of the champagne?"

He complied while remarking, "you are too far away now."

So, with one fluid movement, she turned and melted into his arms; the glasses clinked gently, and lips caressed in a kiss.

She never tired of the bubbles, the flavour of the sparkling delight, as well as the kiss that followed.

Her eyes remained open and she felt the familiar warmth as her head rested in the crook of his shoulder, each a perfect fit, each like a piece in a puzzle, they just connected together and made a perfect whole.

He took a sip and she felt his neck move as he swallowed, then resting the base of her glass on his chest she watched the ebb and flow of his breathing.

Feeling the damp of a single tear edge out the corner of her eye. "No!" she exclaimed.

"No?" the soft reply

At once she realised she had voiced her fight.

"I know we said…" she hesitated. "But…" she could not find the words to continue so she just melted closer into his embrace.

As he felt the warmth of her, he too remembered the first time he had seen her. She was at a tiny table with two friends as they shared fish and chips, the vinegar ran out and she was the one who went to the bar. He walked straight there and when the bottle arrived he reached for it, their fingers just barely grazed but he felt an intense pulse, a shock, and to this day he could not describe it, he just knew that she was the only one for him. As she gazed up at him with clear sky-blue eyes, he literally felt the warmth of her smile as if the sun were reaching out to warm him. He had moved back to the corner and watched as she returned to the table, waiting to see if she would look back to where they had been standing, he had seen her glance but not look around, and in that moment of her sincere shyness, he knew that his life would never be the same again.

At thirty-nine he was young for the number of years he had already been a professor, but he was used to that, the youngest in school for top marks, the youngest to graduate, the youngest with honours, yet with all of this he felt old at times, most recently when he could not sleep and would take a walk in the early hours of the morning. The air would always be crisp and often as not, there would be a moon when he would walk from his flat or near the university campus down the street when the pubs were closing and over the small bridge to the park. He would reflect on his staid and uneventful life, neither sad nor happy.

Stirring gently, she asked "What are you remembering?" As usual keen to his inner thoughts.

He smiled, "Our second date."

"No." she contradicted.

"It's not fair how well you know me!"

"I was thinking of my life just before we met, and… then of our second date."

"Ah yes," her smile deepened, "you wanted to impress with your culinary technique."

"I had to; remember you couldn't cook at all." he laughed

"Eggs," she protested, "I was, and still am, very good at eggs."

"Yes," he admitted, "you are very good at eggs."

"Oh yes, I remember " she sat up giggling almost bumping his glass, "The sausage, sizzled and almost caught fire, there was lots of smoke and we had to open the windows of which there were only two and one tiny skylight, and it was snowing and it melted and made a puddled mess! You were hilarious with a smoky apron, your moustache singed, and eyebrows black." She continued to giggle and her raven hair covered her like a billowing cloud.

He caught his breath, her laughter never changed it was always melodic, at least to him. He tried to look offended but could not, her laughter was contagious.

Within two months they had married, shocking friends on both sides, he a thirty-nine-year-old professor, she a ninteen-year-old student. Neither cared, even if it did go against his conservative nature, he had never considered an alternative, they were perfect together. He brought caution she brought spontaneity, he brought frugality she brought generosity, and they both brought love, a deep, abiding, loyal, passionate love, that all of their friends enjoyed, and others envied.

As a popular and well-regarded professor, he was asked to travel to different posts, Spain, France, Canada, and New Zealand, while she wrote children's books. The years passed quickly, and after six she felt the stirrings of their own child, it was a warm summer day when he arrived home and she ran into his arms to tell him he would soon be a father. He had twirled her around the room, before falling into a loving heap on the bed giggling together.

The laughter and happiness lasted exactly five months and two weeks, followed by many months of tears, a boy, too tiny, too frail to live and with the sadness of knowing that there would be no more.

"We never did decide on a name, did we?" she asked, yet again reading the memory in his face.

"I had thought Alexander, after your father, maybe?" his fingers pinched the top of his nose between his eyes to stop the tears.

"I had thought Phillip. A boy should be named after his father."

He pulled her close feeling her long lithe body as it moulded into his own.

She felt his steady heartbeat and curled into his embrace, just as she always had, it was warm, it was instinctive, like breathing, it just happened .She and he shared love and life.

The jangle of the phone interrupted. She groaned softly as he pulled her into a sitting position, gently unwrapping himself from the warm embrace to address the unwanted interruption. She curled into a comfortable ball and watched his tall lean frame draw to its full height and walk to the phone.

"Hello?"

She listened to the one-sided conversation and watched his face as each feature changed First a furrowed brow, next eyebrows drawn together, and then as he stroked his chin in reflection a light coming into his eyes, and finally, the small wrinkles curled around his eyes as he laughed showing the dimple on his left cheek.

She must remember to kiss that again, before…

"Yes, that's right, you have it. No, that's no problem I understand it's always best to verify." He hesitated, turned and winked, she caught her breath, no matter how many times in their life together, when he looked at her that way, she always felt it in her heart, a sudden start, a warmth, a momentary joy.

"No. No, really, that's fine. Yes, that's right, we'll be back in London in a week, and we'll all have dinner. Yes, yes." he rolled his eyes, shrugged his shoulders and turned with a final comment to end the call.

"Are we on holiday or not?" she queried

In a moment he was at her side. "Of course!"

She smiled and kissed his dimple, "Champagne?"

He stood, smiled and bowed, "Your wish is my command," and with a small flourish presented a second bottle for her approval.

Dinner, as usual, was served on the balcony, and as they watched the warm sun slip into the cool blue horizon, their fingers touched and played one upon the other, a gentle tingling.

"Do you never tire of returning here?" She asked, although she already knew the answer.

"I never tire of returning here with you, and I only worry that you will tire of me." He gazed at his wife, his lover, his friend.

She giggled. "And I always wondered why you never tried to change me, to make me more responsible and less…"

"Less spontaneous, to make you less fun, open, genuine, loving… less than what you are? How could I ever do that? How could I ever change what I love most about you?"

She held up her hand. "Stop! Stop! I love what you say but you promised no silly compliments!"

He bowed his head for a moment, then lifted it and winked. "Alright no more Mr Nice Guy, you are officially challenged to chess."

"What are the stakes? Just so I know what I am going to lose. You know I never win." She pouted.

He smiled. "Yes, but you always play."

She loved to play but he was always better, a chess champion in school he rarely lost. She insisted he teach her, and he complied, when he was once foolish enough to let her win, the tirade that followed prevented that pretence ever again. So many nights they would play in front of the fireplace, drink brandy, talk, and every game would last a very long time.

She returned his smile, "Tonight I am wearing lots of jewelry, you will have to work very, very hard to win."

The next morning the chaise was once again on the balcony and she lay back soaking up the warm rays of the early morning sunshine sipping the strong coffee she so loved.

He lay next to her, both turning to watch the sun as it started its golden assent, savouring the moment, striving to live in, enjoy, and memorise each and every moment, as they would all soon end.

He could not think of a future of lonely sunrises, lonely sunsets, of days and nights that did not include those hypnotic blue eyes, the laughter, the constant surprise that was her.

"Do you know that some people go an entire lifetime and never know what we have known? What we have felt? And we have had thirty years, that is so many lifetimes." She lifted her sunglasses and turned her to gaze at him.

It amazed him, how so often she would know exactly what he was thinking and so answer his unasked query.

Twenty years younger she was supposed to be the one to outlive the man she loved and married. Yet she was the one, who had only days to live in this life, moments before she would be ashes and dust and memories, and at sixty-nine he would have to go onto a with life without her. He could not bear to think of it, so he did not, and once again she knew.

"If you don't behave yourself, I shall come back to haunt you." She smiled

He turned to gaze upon the face he loved. "Promise?"

Midnight

The cold hard beach gave way as the ocean rushed over my feet, and my toes wriggled in the squishy sand erupting tiny volcanos of wet goo. Sandy sludge encased my ankles and mesmerised in the glow of a full moon I become a part of this solitary midnight scene.

Sunset

Phillip stared at the golden orb slipped into darkness and as he watched the sunset, he remembered *The Sunset*... He always referred to it as *The Sunset* because there never was one in the last sixty-five years that could replicate its beauty.

She was sixteen when he first met Katherine and her quiet beauty filled his soul.

He had come to the small villa on the lake to finish his convalescence, it had been a long illness and doctors said he needed time and quiet, so he decided to visit the home of his grandfather's friend.

The journey in the old coach was long and uncomfortable and he arrived on a moonless night when the rain shut out the world. The next morning, he awoke to sunlight, and so heartened he rang for a servant who soon came to attend to him quickly and efficiently. As he gazed out the window, he admired the rich colours, the deep reds of the homes, bright green trees contrasting to the dark blue of the lake which was dotted with small pink islands. The beauty of the scene created an unfamiliar desire to explore the charm of this enigmatic country.

Soon there was a soft knock on the door and sweet words of a morning greeting.

"Maggie is here to give your breakfast but I wanted to make sure you are comfortable, and all is well?"

He turned to see a vision of beauty he did not think could exist in a mortal woman, she had long dark waves framing a perfect heart-shaped face with soft blue-grey eyes.

The words were spoken so softly and sweetly they felt like a soft caress and he was filled with a sense of her warm nature.

The maid followed directly behind her carrying a tray brimming with breakfast delights familiar to his home, bacon, ham, eggs, toast, and strong black coffee. She placed it on a table by the sun filled window then she curtsied and fled her long skirts whispering her goodbye.

Katherine smiled and with a tiny courtesy introduced herself, "When you have finished, if you feel well enough, please come to the garden and see papa, I believe you met him a while ago?"

"Yes, once a long time ago, he knew my grandfather well."

She hesitated for a moment then turned back to say, "I do hope you will find health in your body and your heart while you are here."

An hour later she asked, "Grandfather, will he come to the garden?"

"Of course, he will child you invited him."

“Grandpapa!"

As Phillip entered the garden he was once again surprised by the vibrancy of the colours. Purples, pinks and crisply cut green hedges that presented the contradiction in a chaos of colour, and a disciplined design reflecting in the final glow of the setting sun.

Katherine rose from the table holding out both hands and kissing both his cheeks quickly before leading him forward to the elegantly dressed white-haired man.

He bowed respectfully then extended his hand, "I am most honoured, Lord Montrose, and I thank you for your kind hospitality."

Lord Montrose gripped the young man's hand, with his own gnarled fingers and was confused by the feeling of such smooth skin in one of middle years.

"How many years has it been?" he asked as the blind eyes settled in the direction of Phillip.

"Please sit my boy, sit. Katherine let us enjoy another of your coffee delights."

Phillip felt the old man's unfocussed gaze return to him, and in his heart, he was almost sad to know that he was neither the man they thought and the last one they would ever know.

Story of Hope

Remember we shared a path for a time
And your life as such was combined with mine

The terror you felt from foot to head
And blood covered the bodies of the dead

Your dark brown eyes beseeched
Your hand outstretched and reached

Your eyes held mine and spoke of pain
With a heart that knew not whom to blame

He came and struck you from behind
An angry brutish man so blind

To the tenderness kindness and care
That should have been yours to bear

Your intelligence and beauty was wrought
Packaged only to be sold and bought

But I was there to give you one gift
To see you stand tall and lift

Your free eyes to the skies above
Unbound unshackled and free to love

The path we shared a single day
I learned so much and had to stay

For when you thought you could no longer cope
It was in that moment came your gift of Hope

And while this moment seemed so fleeting
It was simply just our very first meeting

That now through all the trials and despair
You must now feel that I am always there

And that I will continue to grow in your heart
And you shall know we never will part

And it's because you're strong
You will right the wrong

That you fight for the old and the young
To know that soon the day will come

When the freedom and rights of some
Will soon be shared by everyone

Remember there is much yet to behold
With your courage and a hidden strength untold

And remember we shared that path for a time
And from then your life was combined with mine

Remember with Hope there is always a way
And within your heart I always will stay

Hot Chocolate

She peered through the window. He was only five minutes late but that rarely happened. He was always so punctual and organised.

Finally, he arrived and performed his usual ritual sitting at the corner table next to the window facing the sea. He pulled the paper out of his knapsack and laid it at the far end, he then pulled a small clock he used as a timer and set it on the other corner, he then pulled the blue pen out of his shirt pocket, it was an old fashioned fountain pen that happened never to leak (probably too afraid) Serena smiled to herself as he fulfilled his usual routine.

The server approached as soon as he was finished.

"The usual Anthony?"

"Yes, please Helen," he smiled and small crinkles framed the corner of his hazel eyes.

She returned the smile and left the white linen napkin just to his right.

"Actually, Helen may I please have whipped cream? I ... I have a small celebration today." He glanced up and looked directly into her eyes.

Disconcerted for a moment Helen hesitated and then as the light dawned her smile widened. "I believe you do Anthony."

As she turned to go and place the order, the familiar fragrance of vanilla and cinnamon filled his nostrils. He breathed deeply and considered how much he would miss this. The familiar… the safe.... the secure. Suddenly life was unknown, it was filled with a strange tingling, a future that was open to creation, a blank book upon which he was going to write. Not the expectation of the day-to-day familiar routine, but the unwritten word, the people yet to meet, the opportunities yet to unfold.

Selena watched the emotions play across his face and felt a single tear. No longer would he come to the corner table, no longer would he chat, drink hot chocolate, and feel the sun upon his face.

She stood up and turned - forgetting for a moment the mirror on the wall.... reflected in it were a set of dark eyes revealing the sadness of a great loss.

"Madame?"

"Yes, Helen?"

"You know this is his last visit?"

Helen held her breath knowing she should not ask and did not have the right to ask.

"Yes, Helen."

"Madame? I only wonder?"

"Yes, Helen... as do I." Selena turned from her reflection, walked to the stand lifted the designer coat and drew it around her shoulders.

She stopped, her gaze once more resting on the figure in the corner. This was the last moment and she wanted to treasure it. Suddenly he glanced up and looked directly into her eyes, there was no recognition, no hate no love just the momentary glance from someone across the room.

Selena turned and walked out the door, chilled with the sudden cold blast.

Helen returned to the small table in the corner with the hot chocolate under a tower of whipped cream.

"Just as requested."

"To perfection." Replied Anthony and as he touched the cane, he realised the white colour was the same as the sugary white of the whipped cream.

He smiled knowing that soon all the variations of white and every other colour were in his future, yet for the moment it was still dim, but not completely dark as it had been. He wondered who had paid for it all? It was an anonymous donation that provided his gift of sight, provided for the specialist to be flown in from another country, his innovative and experimental surgery, and the weeks of follow-up care.

After his first sip of creamy hot chocolate, and wiping the luscious whipping cream from the tip of the nose he came back to the present and reached for the so familiar crossword puzzle with its customary bumps and the pen that made holes rather than leaving trails of ink.

He heard the sea and looked up focusing on the frothy white waves that curled against the shore, and smiled as he once again delighted in the knowledge soon he would enjoy seeing those variations of whites after living in a world of darkness, soon he would appreciate, but until then.....

She turned and slipped on oversized sunglasses and sighed wiping away the single tear knowing that many more of both sadness and joy would follow. She glanced through the window once more, he had his father's eyes, and now he would see all the beauty in life just as his father had.

Day at the Beach

Joe help your sister finish that sandcastle we're leaving soon! Mark, I told you to put suntan lotion on! Now you're purple! Annie don't forget to tie your bikini top before you stand up! Maggie get that icky sandy seaweed out of your mouth! Just another day at the beach…

Heartbeat

She gazed at the rich purple flowers and proceeded to cut each one with care as if the gentler she was the less it would hurt the flower, and briefly wondered if flowers actually did have feelings.

There was a small whisper of the door opening, before the deep yet gentle tones of her butler's inquiry. "Mrs. Holmes?"

"Yes, Watson."

"There is a" he hesitated over the next word, "lady… caller and she insists you know her." The sniff that followed this statement implied his disbelief.

"Watson, you are so judgemental!" And laughed, nodding her assent to see the visitor while adding, "oh, Watson would you please grind up the flowers and do be careful, remember it must be a pure extraction."

He inclined his head in assent.

She handed the basket of Foxglove clippings to him, along with her gloves and cutter.

A moment later a tiny woman with greying hair and sad blue-grey eyes entered the garden.

Sheena Holmes turned, and it took a minute to recognise the face of her childhood friend as she had aged much over the years, and then embraced the fragile form.

Quickly covering her surprise Sheena greeted her old friend.

"Elizabeth what a lovely surprise to see you after all these years."

The small figure reluctantly pulled herself from the embrace staring up at the woman who was only two years younger but looked decades younger. The years definitely did not show on the clear fair skin, brilliant emerald eyes, and black wavy hair.

"You, you haven't changed at all," observed Elizabeth.

"Oh, well we've all earned our experiences and wear our years."

"I think someone else is wearing yours."

Sheena waived away the compliment and proceeded to guide her guest to the table, at which tea, scones with cream and jam, as well as finger sandwiches that had quickly and quietly appeared.

As she poured tea and served her guest Sheena examined the previously beautiful features of her old friend. The once bright blue-grey eyes were now opaque, more grey than blue and surrounded with tiny wrinkles, while the vibrant honey blonde hair was now streaked with grey and had been tucked into a feeble chignon. While Elizabeth had always been petite, she now seemed shrunken and the boney fingers which held the fine china teacup shook slightly.

Finally, Elizabeth looked directly into Sheena's dark and mesmerising eyes "You do know why I'm here, don't you?"

Sheena gave a small shrug in response and raised the perfectly arched eyebrows.

"We were once close friends! We're almost the same age, how can you do this?" Elizabeth exclaimed.

Sheena looked at her old friend with a completely blank expression. "Do what? What could I possibly have done to offend and hurt you so?"

"Robert, it's Robert, he's my son!" And at that moment Elizabeth pulled a photograph out of her bag.

It was a small black and white with the posed photo of a woman sitting and the man standing attentively on her right a shot that was so popular at the moment. The back had the photographers stamp and the date 1st of April 1912, taken only a few days before.

Sheena took the photo and saw the reflection of herself with her new young lover, and the flicker of recognition was so quick as to be missed by the small woman, despite her intense stare.

"What if anyone should find out? It is an embarrassment for me but more especially for you." Suddenly the opaque eyes held a sharp and shifty look.

"I am so so sorry Elizabeth, I had no idea, I mean I knew he was younger, but to be your son! Of course, I will accede to your wishes."

Sheena once again drew her friend in a close embrace, but the smile did not reach the dark and now stormy expression in her eyes.

"Is there anything else I can do for you? Is there any other help I can provide?" Sheena knew the answer before she even asked the question She always knew it was a plea for money.

Elizabeth touched the corner of her mouth with the delicate napkin and replied. "Well, I wouldn't say no to a little help."

Sheena stood, and quickly deciding what must be done rang for her butler.

"Watson, please call a hansom cab for Mrs. Bridge," while waving away the objections of her former friend. "Also, would you please bring a box of the new chocolates we have, and Watson please make sure it is the purple box."

Turning back Sheena said, "I do love the colour purple, it is so vibrant." And once again she smiled.

"Watson will visit you in just a few days, and I am sure that the financial aspect will be acceptable to you. Please know that you have nothing to worry about, indeed I shall never see Robert again, so long as we live."

The tiny woman smiled her appreciation, clutching her bag, not yet realising that Sheena had slipped the photo into the hidden pocket of her long skirt.

"As a matter of fact, Elizabeth, why don't you take a little holiday? I was going to sail to America in a few days, and I can no longer go. You could take Robert with you."

Sheena waited for the response and then added quickly, "That's it all set, the ship sails in a few days on the 10th of April from Southampton for New York and it should be a quick sailing, it's a new ship and this is its maiden voyage."

"No, no, no, I couldn't," protested Elizabeth.

"I insist, I was wondering what to do with the tickets anyway."

Goodbyes were said and Sheena pressed the purple box into Elizabeth's hands. "Just a small bon voyage gift between friends, I know that chocolate does the heart so much good."

Indeed, the box was heart-shaped. Moments later the cab whisked away the old friend, and Mrs. Holmes once again rang for her butler. "I am so glad we have a lovely full garden this year, though I must admit we are using more of the foxglove this year than last year. However, there is still a large quantity left. I do not think we will run out."

"Yes, madame." Replied the butler, bowing ever so slightly. "I shall also have to order more purple boxes, and I assume you wish them to be heart-shaped as well."

"Of course! Yes, please do Watson. You know it is extraordinary really, that such a simple beautiful flower can stop a heart so quickly." Sheena turned and with an ever so small smile and a wicked wink at her butler.

"Please bring me a sherry Watson."

"With pleasure Madame."

"Oh, what time is Governor Holmes expected?"

"About seven o'clock, Mrs. Holmes. Will you wish to have dinner at the usual time?"

"Yes, Watson."

Days later Mrs. Holmes was once again in the garden sipping tea and reading the paper aloud. Of particular interest was the story of a middle-aged widow woman traveling alone who was among the passengers who drowned when the ship hit an iceberg in the Atlantic and sank. As her glittering green eyes continued to scan the account Sheena Holmes felt her heart skip a beat as Robert pulled her against his chest and caressed her lips with his own. She briefly wondered if the chocolates had performed their task before the ship was engulfed in its own watery death.

Memories

You know how it is; you walk into a restaurant, it is crowded, popular and you weave your way through the tables. You flow because this is where you have lived all your life, a small town on the coast, popular throughout the summer, but still secluded.

His hand guides your waist into the seat, not needed but warm and welcoming. Philipe flourishes the menu, which you know by heart.

He gazes for a moment, and then looks at you, well not really at you as all the rest have done, he looks into you, and then his black eyes flash with humour.

He says still gazing at you, "Do you know? I don't know."

Philipe hesitates only a moment and with a small and self-deprecating smile, "I would not presume to …."

"Please do," he says.

Then Philipe fades away.

He lights your cigarette, and you look into those black eyes and wonder, but only for a moment.

"You do know that you are the most fascinating and enchanting woman?" He smiles, although his sea-green eyes are suddenly mysterious and hard to read.

"How should I answer that?" You query. "Either I sound too conceited or too erudite?"

His smile deepens.

He puts his hand in his pocket and pulls out a small object and asks for your hand and with gentle care slips the diamond ring on the third finger of your left hand. A breath escapes, and then you nod your head knowing that whatever the future holds it will include the loving and much-loved face before you.

"Grandma! Where are you?" The incessant yammering of high-pitched voices pierce and brake the quiet.

"I am here," she says unfolding from the quiet of her hiding place for hide and seek, no matter the generation, no matter the child they had never been able to find her when she hid beneath the quilt, it was almost magic. I suppose it was magic, it was the wedding quilt she had made all those years ago. Reminding her of a life filled with a pair of beautiful black eyes, of stormy seas, and of a love so very long ago.

"Grandma! Where are you!" Again demanded young Alexander looking up at me as if I am not there, and perhaps it is because as I look at him, I am not there, I am in a place long ago of love, and warmth and a place to which I will soon return.

Mesmerised

She felt the foamy white salty water rush over her feet and then recede back into the vast ocean begging her to follow its beckoning whisper. Her footsteps squished as she stepped through the sodden sand, and yet again felt the flow going higher up her leg, so she followed. Mesmerised.

Twin Glasses

Peter usually woke up just after daylight and today was no different as he stuck his nose above the warmth of the feather duvet. At home, he knew if it was cold, he would have to rush and pull on his robe, but when visiting Gran he knew his robe would be warm and toasty, and today was no different. Wrapped in the cozy robe he crept down the stairs remembering to miss the second to the last step with its distinctive creak, and slowly peeked around the corner of the doorway.

As sunlight streaked into the kitchen it cast a warm almost angelic glow around his Gran, who without turning said, "you know Peter if you help the breakfast will be done very soon."

She turned and he saw the beautiful clear blue eyes, snow white curls and loving expression which he adored so much.

She offered a huge mitten, "now if you are very careful, you won't get burned."

He stuffed his hand into the mitten and pulled down the oven door, while Gran put in the first batch of cinnamon rolls.

"Thank you, Peter."

"Welcome Gran." And knew even at this young age he felt the importance of this simple ceremony that was the preparation of the gooey delights. Handing back the kitchen mitten he accepted his cuddle and the lift up to the counter to watch as she continued the baking process.

She turned back to the worktop and swiftly rolled out the dough into a long rectangular, adding butter, cinnamon, sugar, and then curling the dough until it soon resembled a long caterpillar. With an expert eye, she cut it in half, half again, and again until there were twenty faultless rolls, each one displaying a perfect pinwheel of flavour.

At that moment a sharp stab of sunlight pierced through the window and struck the wine glasses sitting on the top shelf adjacent to the window.

He knew that these were no ordinary wine glasses, he knew that they were made of the same stained glass that decorated the local church. As the sun reflected and bounced off of them it created a prism filling the kitchen in a rainbow of colour.

Oblivious to the rainbow his Gran turned and offered a pinky slick with the gooey cinnamon sweetness that was encased in the buns.

"Gran, why do those glasses make a rainbow?"

Annie turned and gazed at her grandson, "Peter you know the story."

"Gran, why do those glasses make a rainbow?" He asked again insisting on hearing the story he already knew by heart.

"The glasses make a rainbow because your grandfather knew that when he and I found each other it was like finding the treasure at the end of a rainbow, and so he had those glasses made for us when we married."

She paused remembering the moment he gave them to her, ensuring that the sun struck the glasses and creating the first of many rainbows and loving memories they were to share

She continued with the story, "they are twin glasses, each is a perfect partner to the other, just like your grandfather and me." She paused for a moment, "you know Peter you are not only named after him you are also quite like him."

He did not know if it was a question or a statement, but he knew that he felt good about it; and just at that moment the sun once again burst into the room and suffused it all the colours of the rainbow, and he knew in his heart that the real treasure at the end of the rainbow was in this tiny kitchen, with the warm smell of cinnamon and the love of a wonderful Gran.

The Inheritance

The rain pelted against the window and ran down in cruel angry streaks. Jasmine gazed unseeing not even trying to focus but just imagining the drops blended together creating the illusion of the glass melting. She sipped the red Bordeaux and bit into the dark chocolate with small sharp white teeth. Now that Robert was dead, she would have to find a new lover, younger and with more money.

The phone buzzed against the glass tabletop, the face she dreaded appeared on the screen.

"Hello?"

"Why does it always sound like a question when you answer the phone?" asked clipped London accent which held the hint of a something more elusive.

Jasmine shivered, "I don't have all the money yet."

"Ahhh I believe she is a bit testy tonight, my lady? Well not to worry, I do realize you have, ummm, suffered recent…financial losses."

"How kind you are." she bit her lower lip to stop from saying anything more sarcastic.

"I am not an unreasonable man, as you well know."

Jasmine waited.

"We could come to an alternative arrangement?" The smooth voice deepened.

She smiled to put a light tone in her voice that was not there. "Well, I would not consider you having to do without the proper financial remunerations. Give me a few days and I'll have the rest."

"Don't forget to add the late fee and then we'll be fine." His tone was like silk and made Jasmine sit up her green eyes lighting the dark in anger.

"Not to worry." she clicked the phone before saying what she so desperately wanted to say which was to tell him to go drop dead and go directly to hell. She shook her head her raven hair waving to and fro as she tried to focus.

A shaft of light broke through the clouds to illuminate the library for a split second before the clouds and rain returned.

Jasmine bent her head, there were only her grandmother's necklace and her father's ring left, and she knew she would die before selling her father's ring, it was all she had left of him.

A soft knock on the door roused her from her worried thoughts. "Come in," she said, unfolding from her position on the sofa.

Tall and slim she towered over the maid who appeared.

"Sorry miss, but it's your brother, he's asking for you."

"Thank you, Marianna, I'll be right up."

Jasmine turned back to the windows as a flash of lightning created a black and white photo of the large comfortable library, dotted with the leather sofas, chairs and wall to ceiling shelves of old books and manuscripts. It had been her father's favourite room, as it was hers.

I wish I could just crawl up and go to sleep and never wake up, she thought, reflecting that it would be a lovely way to spend eternity, before closing the door behind her.

***

Shaun opened the brown paper parcel and viewed the contents with suspicious eyes, finally, he nodded.

"Looks okay."

"Okey dokey, but jus' so ya know this here is the best constructed in the business." Nodded Leonard with his poor diction and puppy dog sad eyes. His head was bobbing up and down like a bobble dog and his greasy dark hair flopped in sticks back and forth as he nodded.

Shaun pulled the roll out of his pocket and peeled off fifteen one hundred-pound notes.

"As long as it does the job, I don't care how it was built." His steel grey eyes raked over Leonard. "Why don't you spend a bit of this cash on a shower?"

"It's not good for my skin! Besides I don't stink." Leonard's scrawny fingers grabbed the bills and stuffed them into his pocket.

Shaun had already turned his tall figure away from the skeletal Leonard, not really caring what he did, knowing he would get his money back.

"Lemme know when you need sumpin' else." And with those parting words, Leonard headed for the staircase but never reached them.

***

"Bruce, honey?" Jasmine whispered the words not enough to wake but enough to let him know that she was there.

"Sis?"

"I'm here."

"I'm sorry." Bruce turned his head toward Jasmine, but his eyes remained closed.

"What for honey? You haven't done anything but lie here and be lazy." Jasmine put a light tone in her voice.

"That's why." The pale features faintly lit as he tried to smile, but the energy was not there and the life force was rapidly leaving.

A tear slid down her cheek and Bruce opened dark jade unfocused eyes.

He held up his hand and Jasmine curled her fingers into his, just as they had done since they were children. She pulled his hand close and rested it against her cheek. Although the room was almost dark, she could still see his small smile. The fine chiseled cheekbones, the perfect eyebrows and the nose, that although had once been broken, still was aquiline.

"I'm sorry because I am leaving you with such a mess. That I won't be here to help."

"Nonsense! You are not getting out of this!"

This time he did smile, and it lit the face in a spasm of beauty. Jasmine caught her breath, he could not die, she would not allow it! First father, then mother, and now her beloved younger half-brother, she could not bear the thought.

"This is one thing you cannot talk your way out of, or control, or change, I am sorry to say." His hand tightened in hers as the spasm of pain passed through this frail body.

***

Shaun nodded to himself, it was all coming together quite well, just a few more days and she would be dead, and all those lovely millions would be his. He closed his eyes to try and shut out the memory of her and shook his head back and forth. He had never loved or hated anyone as much. He drew a ragged breath and lit a cigarette, pulling hard to fill his lungs with smoke.

He reached for the bottle and drained the last dregs straight until it was done and, as he straightened up, he caught a glimpse of himself in the broken mirror and saw that he definitely needed a shave, and those bags under his eyes weren't helping his look, but he knew in a few days when he was in the sun with a blonde and a bottle he would forget, at least for a while.

***

His eyes closed and his breathing slowed, she held on tight to his hand as if her strength and her will could course through him and give him new life.

Tears slid down Jasmine's cheek landing on the now limp hand that that she held within her own.

***

Shaun peered into the mirror as he shaved, the beard was coming off, but the wrinkles remained, hell they were grooves. Some women called him distinguished, some handsome, some well-worn, he just felt tired and old.

He closed his eyes and opened them again, and to his dismay the reflection had not changed, in fact, if possible his eyes looked even redder.. He sighed and finished his shave and shower. By the time he dressed it was eight o'clock. The new gun fit nicely into the back holster and he stood back to make sure the look was complete. The new custom navy suit, crisp white shirt, and blue silk tie set off his dark good looks and sharpened the steely darkness in his grey eyes. He looked at the box again, opened it and pulled out the silver cigarette case slipping it into his inside pocket. It fit perfectly into the line of his suit's slim look.

The countdown was official, two more days. Just forty eight hours. He took one last swallow of whiskey and walking up the stairs, turned briefly to toss the matches into the cellar then jogged quickly up the stairs knowing he had thirty seconds before the whole house would go up leaving behind the crumpled, unconscious heap that was the boney smelly Leonard. He smiled for the first time in weeks, he was removing any evidence that he had ever been there, he left no one that could lead a trail directly to him. He knew his work would continue all night, and that was how he wanted it, he wanted to savour his revenge to ensure that she was made to suffer and to know that he was the one to make her suffer and that by tomorrow he would be winging his way to paradise. He heard the blast as the house went up in a blaze, but didn't turn around, there was not point. He always believed in looking forward not ever back.

***

The funeral was small, the ceremony short and the dinner too long. Jasmine's head ached with a pain that several pills and two bottles of champagne could not assuage.

Finally, the day was over and she was left in the large lonely house that would soon be dispossessed of her along with everything she owned. At least she would not have to worry about money for a short time, the sale would keep her going, but she was definitely going to have to address the situation, but not now, for now, she had to turn and cry into the pillow that held so many tears and which soon would also be a memory.

***

He pulled at the string and the knot came loose as did the bikini top, Daisy moaned and turned in his arms her hands curling into his hair and pulling his head down to her own.

Shaun paused to look into the sea green eyes of his conquest and then closed his own as he fought to forget the blue eyes that haunted him whenever he held a woman. She moaned again and moved her lips, her perfect figure pressed against his own and he decided to forget, he would forget, she would make him forget and then his fingers tangled her hair and pulled her head back and he crushed her figure into his as if to process her every fibre of her being.

The next morning Daisy awoke and listened closely, she could hear his soft snores and even breathing. He was troubled and she knew it, she also knew he loved someone that he hated. That was always the worst when a man loved something or someone he could not have. She slowed her breathing and turned gently from her left side to lie on her back and listened to make sure he was still asleep. She peered at him from under her lashes in case he awoke suddenly, he had such long lovely lashes and lips that were strong but full, and in sleep, he looked so much younger than when he was awake with all those furrowed looks and wrinkles around his eyes.

She hated to admit that a part of her wanted him so much, just to have him to herself, and while she was the one he came to most, she was not the only one. She scrunched her eyes closed to try and stop the tears, it wasn't her job to cry, her job was to give pleasure, and she did it better than most because she always knew what they wanted and how to give that to them. It was so much more than sex, that was the easy part, it was knowing what they really wanted. But with Shaun it was different, she knew she was a substitute, that any other woman would be a substitute. But hell, she was definitely going to give that damned ghost a run for her money. She turns toward him and moaned softly, and tickled his lips with her tongue, and soon possessed the only part she knew she could have.

***

Shaun revved the motorcycle as he circled the drive, the sun had been up for around an hour and he had been on the road about four. He never minded getting up early when he was on the road with the bike, watching the sun come up, feeling the wind and of course there was always the speed.

He kicked the stand, pulled off the helmet and looked up, God he hadn't been here in ten years. Time passed but things never changed.

The door opened.

"Good morning Master Shaun."

"God .... just call me Shaun, I'm no one's master." Then he smiled realising that when it came to Daisy, he might be a master.

"Yes, Master Shaun."

"Is my sister awake?"

"Just, sir. Coffee and breakfast will be served in the conservatory this morning."

Shaun tossed the helmet to the butler and headed through the doors.

Everything was in the backpack *Too bad* he thought looking around just realising just how beautiful the house was, but it was not what he wanted, he wanted the twenty million pounds that she was worth. He laughed to himself, the policy had been by their father years ago and she knew nothing about it, just as well.

He strolled in careful to not jiggle the container, would not be right to have it go off while he was still here.

Tudor Times

Mary lit the candle and let the meagre light guide her to the door and allowing her eyes to adjust from the dark to the misty light, and turned the handle very slowly to ensure as little noise as possible .

Compared to her small and fire-warmed room, the hallway was cold. She did not care Richard would be waiting, and her heart skipped a beat. She pulled the cloak around her shoulders and felt to ensure that the jewel-filled pouch was still attached to her waist under the unfamiliar garments. She felt the weight and was reassured about her future.

The king had made her decision to leave sooner than she wished, but she knew she could not give in to his advances, his appetite for food and women were well known, but she had remained pure for her own reasons, she would only be with the man she would marry and no one, not even the king, would take that from her.

She made her way quickly as she was not encumbered by the numerous layers of a lady's dress, she was delighted with her idea of borrowing her page's clothes.

Having spent six months in London her inquisitive nature allowed her extensive knowledge of the home she was visiting. The turret stairs were not far from her room and led to a lower floor which in turn led to the landing place for the small boats that ran up and down the Thames.

She moved silently guarding the flame. Soon the tapestry loomed before her and she drew it back to reveal the half-sized door. Removing the key from her pocket she pushed it in and slowly turned it to the left listening for it to release, she heard the click and a moment later she slipped through the door and blew out the candle.

Feeling the cold stone on her right she stood for a minute to allow her large blue eyes to become accustomed to the dark. In a short time, she was gliding down the stairs keeping her hand on the right-side stone to ensure her balance.

Mary heard a click behind her and stopped. There was a small cold whisper of air which raised the hair on the back of her neck. She hesitated, and in the next moment, she felt another whisper of air as silk wafted in front of her and then quickly pulled against her neck. Instinctively her hands reached up to claw at the material drew her life from her. She flailed then saw blackness as she went limp, then nothing.

Two hours later Mary, now Marie, felt warming hands rubbing her wrists and caressing her forehead. She had a brief question in her mind *was this what heaven felt like?* Then came the smell of oak, candle wax, and wine to bring her to her to her senses.

"I was so worried about you." The familiar voice whispered against her ear.

She smiled and snuggled into his embrace.

"Sorry."

"That was too, too close, I followed him and was only a moment behind! I know the king desired you but to send…" his voice trailed off.

"I have complete faith in you, my love. I know that nothing would have happened, and now we have nothing to fear."

"If it would have…."

She pressed a finger against his lips and looked into his brilliant green eyes.

"Never doubt."

And they melted into each other's arms.

Day of Changes

He sipped the lager and let his gaze rest on the reflection in the long mirror that ran the length of the bar.

She was tucked into the corner and her heart-shaped face reflected the emotions of the book she was reading. Her dark hair just brushed her shoulders as it moved from side to side. He liked watching her expressive face. It was like a movie, sad, pensive, happy, and puzzled. He wondered about the book. What could possibly bring out so many emotions?

He raised the glass to his lips, just ready to take the last swallow when she raised her head and looked directly into the mirror, directly into his eyes, for just a moment and then returned to the page she was reading. He stopped just short of spilling the amber liquid. Her eyes. He had never seen eyes of such vivid dark green. They reminded him of the emerald ring his mother had always worn, of how the facets in the stone would glint different shades of green intensity.

Sam stopped in front of him, finished polishing a glass and slid it onto the overhead rack to join the other glasses.

"She never speaks to anyone, that one."

Sam gazed at him, with one clear eye, the other was half shut, as always with the lid pulled to one side. Disconcerting at first to see one lopsided with a long thin scar, no one knew the story of how it had happened it was just part of Sam.

"You headed home?" Sam interrupted his thoughts.

He put the empty glass on the bar. "No, Sam, I think I'll have another."

"She never speaks to anyone, that one." Sam repeated his statement putting the glass into the washer and putting a clean one under the lager tap.

Paul felt his gaze move to the mirror as if drawn by a magnet. Her dark hair fell to one side of her face and her tiny nose pointed directly at the book she had been reading for the last hour. The glass of red wine had been replaced only once in that time. Her hand always found the stem without her ever raising her eyes, and the long pale fingers rested for a moment before lifting the glass.

Paul turned and saw the small stream of white froth run down one side of the glass once again interrupting his reverie.

"She never…."

Paul holding up his hand stopped Sam, " I know… never speaks to anyone."

Paul took a long drag of the cold liquid feeling it cool his throat and trail down, how he never tired of that first swallow, thousands of pints and still he never tired of that first taste. He put the glass back down noting that it was now half empty. His first sips were getting larger. A flicker of movement drew his gaze back to the dark hair in the corner of the mirror.

Her head was tilted slightly to one side and a half smile played across her lips. Those long fingers had released the glass and ran down the edge of the page stopping at the bottom and then moving one finger flipped the page.

Her smile widened and small creases formed around those intense green eyes. Once again, she raised her head, and he was struck by the piercing emerald gaze. It only lasted a second and the black veil of her hair fell as her head bent over the book once again.

He longed to reach out and tuck the hair behind her ear and caress the pale smooth skin of her cheek. He wondered what passion lay behind those lovely pink lips.

Sam seemed intent on polishing every glass right in front of Paul, chomping on the eternal and everlasting piece of gum.

"What's her name?" Paul wondered and then realised he had spoken the question aloud when Sam replied.

"Ebony." Sam answered.

Paul raised an eyebrow.

"I know, weird huh? Maybe cause her hair is so dark?"

Sam smacked his gum again and reached for another of the never-ending supply of glasses that required polishing.

Paul leaned back, trying to think of a reason to talk to her. Wanting to be drawn closer into those mesmerising green eyes. For a second he gazed at his own reflection, ten years ago he wouldn't have had this problem, blond, blue-eyed, and tall he had never suffered from a lack of female attention, they had said he had rakish good looks.

He took another long sip and put the empty glass on the bar.

"Nother one?"

Paul nodded and briefly wondered how Sam managed to butcher most words.

Then Paul noticed the empty wine glass, his gaze moved to Sam who was rhythmically pulling the handle for the lager.

Without moving an eye from watching the pour Sam stated, "nope, she doesn't take a drink from anyone, said it the first time she came in like she knew men would offer or just send one over to her."

Sam ambled over to the side of the bar to take an order as he waited for the top of the lager to settle,. He poured two drinks, then returned to top it up and set the pint down.

Paul felt the familiar tug of pain near his right rib and grimaced slightly. It wasn't going to get any better, and he raised his glass in a silent toast knowing he didn't really care, enough pints and he wouldn't feel the pain anyway.

"Sam? may I have another please?"

Paul felt the warm softness of her voice melt over him and he couldn't stop his gaze from resting on her. She leaned on the back of the bar stool and the easy grace of her stance reflected years of ballet.

"Miss Ebony, never known you to have more'n two." Sam's face reddened,

"I know Sam, but today is a day of changes." Then she turned the full force of those emerald eyes to rest on Paul.

Skint Knee

"Mama! Mama!" The small voice cut through the silence. "I didn't even cry!"

Miranda opened her eyes to see her young son running up the garden path with a trail of blood running down from his right knee.

She straightened up on the chaise lounge and held out her arms to engulf the small whirlwind that was her son.

"So, let me see the damage."

"Oh mama, it's only a little blood and I didn't even cry." He repeated with pride.

"And what did happen?

Jeremy straightened up on his mother's lap to ensure he had her complete attention.

"Well, I was riding near the old house and paying special attention in case the witch would appear..."

His mother interrupted "There are no witches!!!! I have told you that! And old Mrs. Smith is just a nice old lady!"

Jeremy tried not to roll his eyes at his mother because he knew the rumours in the school that she was a witch, and his mum always thought the best of everyone.

"Mama? May I continue?"

Miranda relented, "Yes."

He squirmed slightly in order to face her and began his story again "So, I was riding near the old house that Mrs. Smith lives in and was looking to see..." he hesitated to gauge his next words, "if she had planted any new flowers." His voice trailed off - even that sounded pathetic to his young ears.

"Jeremy, what have I said about lying?"

"You said my nose would grow long and be that way forever."

"Well, not exactly - but close enough. Lying is very bad, it leaves a mark on you that you cannot see but lives with you forever. So, begin again and this time please tell me the truth." And as she patted his knee, he noticed that there was no more blood and that his small injury had healed as though it had never happened.

Miranda used her finger to tilt his face up and smiled, and as he began to relate the story again, he felt himself tire and slowly curl up into the warmth of his mother's embrace.

Soon afterwards a tall shadow fell over mother and son.

Miranda gazed with love up into the eyes that mirrored the rich emerald colour of their son.

He reached out and she guided the sleeping child safely into his father's embrace. He looked at the knee and tutted. "You are not supposed to be..."

She interrupted, "It was a small skint knee."

He gazed at her trying to put a reproving tone in his voice and failing, "It's not just...."

He sighed then leaned over to graze the lips with a gentle kiss, "I don't know why I even try. You are just too beautiful to argue with."

Miranda smiled and snuggled into the chaise knowing the one next to her would soon be occupied by her husband, lover, and friend. She picked up the phone. "Hello, Auntie Becca."

"Hello child."

"Auntie Becca I think we need to update and renovate your house, apparently the children think you're a witch!"

Miranda heard a giggle on the end of the phone before continuing, "I know, I know, but you have to expect a bit of a problem when you insist on continuing to stay in Salem, I mean, Uncle John brought you here as his bride, in what? 1694?"

Le Chat Noir

As the long slim, pale fingers gently rubbed back and forth Kismet continued his purring, and slowly rubbed his right ear against her. Jonathan placed the glass of red wine on the table in front of his wife and tilted her chin to place a small kiss on the tip of her nose without disturbing the contented cat. Sarina's blue eyes gazed into her husband's and her lips curved into a small smile.

"How did today go?" she inquired.

"Exactly as expected, we shall net about two million," he hesitated then added, "after taxes."

Her smile widened. "You must admit, our initial investment has decidedly paid for itself."

He settled into the deeply cushioned chair and winked. "I must agree with you, and as usual you were quite correct in your assessment of his attributes."

Sarina leaned forward her fingers caressing the stem of the glass before raising it to sip the ruby red liquid.

Kismet mewed at the movement and then settled back into the comfort of his mistress's lap, closing his black eyes in anticipation of the gentle caress and as a prelude to his contented purring.

"I am quite jealous at this moment." Jonathan commented, his dark grey eyes narrowing as he contemplated the black cat.

"I don't know why, you have been in this particular position more often than I can count.

"And I never tire of it." Jonathan unfolded his long legs and leaned forward, arms outstretched to take possession of the ebony feline.

His mobile phone buzzed on the table and during the distraction, Kismet reached out sharp claws to scratch his extended hand.

"Not again!" he exclaimed. "Honestly, I don't know if he is worth the millions!"

Sarina laughed, "Answer the phone, and you know he is!"

She pulled Kismet close into a loving cuddle, rubbing her cheek against his head.

Irritated Jonathan almost barked into the phone. "Hello!"

Suddenly he was attentive for a few minutes and then a smile softened his handsome features.

"Well, well, well. That is good news. We anticipated about two million but four million is decidedly good news."

Sarina's right eyebrow arched questioning the context of the conversation and drew the warmth of the small furry bundle closer into her arms. She heard the click of the phone and waited for the news.

"I don't think we should use Kismet for our projects, we can loan him out and list it as consulting services." He winked once again as he took a long sip from his wine glass.

"Please explain the conversation, what is now worth four million?"

Jonathan dropped into the comfort of the chair and, with his monogrammed handkerchief, dabbed the small amount of blood oozing from the long thin scratches on his left hand next to the sparkling diamond set in his wedding ring.

"Well, it turns out that Kismet was greedier than we expected and got away with two pair of matching diamonds rather than just one. Lady Millicent has just advised the police that there were two sets of diamond earrings stolen rather than just the one set.

Sarina lifted Kismet staring into his ebony eyes, gently shaking him from side to side as his paws tried to swipe at her heart-shaped diamond necklace, his black eyes focused on the flashing rainbow colours of the diamond.

"What are we going to do with you?" she asked him, knowing there would be no answer.

"I think we should feed him a laxative sooner rather than later."

"Well, I agree to that, however, Kismet is part of our family, my family, and I will not share his particular idiosyncrasy with anyone else!"

Jonathan nodded his agreement and sighed, after all, Kismet and his predecessors had been part of Sarina's family for the last century, and in reality, he could only wonder at the luck of having a black cat with a dietary affinity for flawless white diamonds.

Murder at the Seaside

"I told you I wanted no further contact between us." The wind tore the words from David's mouth and bounced them off the craggy rocks.

The black-clad figure smiled in answer.

"There will be no further contact."

The wind continued its assault and yanked black tendrils from David's ponytail, stinging his eyes as they whipped his face. The small figure moved closer raising its right hand. Jonathan blinked trying to focus and tottered as he stepped back. He focused on the gun.

"Why?"

"Don't be ridiculous, you know why."

"It doesn't have to be this way; you know I won't give you any trouble."

As David spoke, he glanced between the barrel and the face, then the memory triggered. "That's the gun I…"

"Yes, very handy. Dangerous to give a deadly weapon as a present, I must say that I do appreciate your … foresight."

David knew he had one last chance and lunged, too late, the gloved hand squeezed the trigger and the bullet found its mark right in the middle of his forehead. David's eyes flashed open in surprise as his tall lean frame collapsed in a heap.

Not quite where I wanted him to land. Oh well, a woman's work is never done, nor always easy. Small gloved hands wrapped around the lapels of the cashmere coat and tugged at the prone figure; it was close enough to the cliff but the uneven ground slowed her progress. A few minutes later the body of Professor David Simmons tumbled into the churning stormy ocean and became a blood-spattered speck as the waves smashed it into the rocks.

Craig's Point was a popular stop on the southern part of the California scenic ocean highway, it jutted out allowing a wide expanse of grass to be used as a picnic area, linear parking ran parallel to the highway and stretches of pitted rocky terrain formed the steep cliff to the ocean below. Surveying the scene, she smiled once more leaning her petite figure against the wind and returned to the small platinum convertible parked on the side of the highway. Scanning the viewing area to see if anyone was watching she pulled out the mobile and stepped into the Ferrari. One key dialled the number.

"Our problem is resolved."

"Excellent."

"I'm staying in the area for a while."

"Do you think that's wise?"

"Oh yes. If I were to leave too suddenly it would definitely raise questions."

"Yes, quite right. Is there anything I can do for you?"

"Not at the moment. Depends on how things proceed, I'll let you know."

"Fine…and you're absolutely certain about how it will go?"

"Yes. I told you, you have nothing to worry about and neither do I."

She clicked end on the keypad.

Placing the gun in the glove compartment, she eased the car onto the highway barely feeling the bump as the car grazed the boulder.

Twenty minutes later the sports car was parked in its reserved spot in the garage, and the petite figure strolled to the elevator smiling in anticipation of a hot bubble bath and a glass of red wine.

All in all, I think it went quite well, she thought smiling

First Moment of Love

Bri cupped the brandy snifter in both hands and leaned against the balcony watching the play of the moon's reflection on the ocean creating a sparkling pathway to the stars. As she raised the brandy to her lips the gold and silver meshed to create a cascade of colours that disappeared again as she lowered the glass. The events of the past few weeks played in her mind like an old black and white silent movie, some garish, some frightening, some emotional, and a few quiet and peaceful like this.

The breeze lifted a few tendrils of hair from the nape of her neck and she felt the warmth of Devlin's breath as he came to stand behind her.

The warmth of him and the coolness of the air made her tingle. She sighed and leaned back against his chest; he wrapped his arms around her holding her in a gentle embrace. They stood together gazing out at the water

She turned to look up at him and at that moment his head bent down and their lips met in a light caressing kiss. The soft and gentle feel of his lips melted any reserve consuming her in a passion so long dormant.

"Brianna?" Devlin whispered against her lips.

Her eyes half opened revelling sapphire slivers in the moonlight. He pulled back to gaze her eyes his dark and questioning.

She felt his heartbeat in a pulsating rhythm that matched her own, her breath quickened as she returned his gaze. She stretched her hands to clasp them around his neck pulling his head toward hers, *please* was all he heard.

The Coffin Train

The rain poured all night long tapping out a droning tune on the metal roof of each village hut. By morning the muddy ground had no support so that when the coffin bearers lined up to begin the procession their sandals squished and sank with each step under the weight of the coffins. Mr Ashong sat in the centre of the village on a high pedestal throne made of the bahonee tree wood, the hardest wood in any of the villages because it is filled with the spirits of strong animals, a lion, a buffalo bull, or an elephant, and is the same wood used for the coffins.

It takes fifty workers one week to cut, shape, and polish each coffin and there are three coffins in every procession. Everyone in the village jostled and crowded into the main street creating flashes of white sarongs, yellow loincloths, and brown oiled skin. This is a traditional procession with eight bearers wearing black loincloth woven from the ebony silkworm, red thrush sandals woven and wrapped around their calves, head shaved and polished with a yellow circle painted on top like a target, black kohl rimmed their eyelids and a gaudy red slash in the centre of their forehead. Each coffin was round like the trunk of a tree and measures twice the height of a man with pegs jutting out to hook the ceremonial carrying poles.

The first coffin looked like the sun god Jungjinra rising in the morning, hand-beaten gold in the shape of the rising sun, each ray studded in diamonds flashing bright white just like a brilliant morning sunrise. As the bearers straightened against the weight of the coffin and pulled their feet out simultaneously from the slimy mud, they began walking down the street in rhythmic unison silently dancing to some unknown and unheard song. A gasp rose as one voice when the morning sunlight struck the coffin and cast a thousand lights, as if the stars in the sky had come down to the earth. Behind young Ramana, Madame Jung and her daughter watched the procession.

"Oh my, Mr Ashong is indeed a man of worth and honour." Observed old Madame Jung.

"Yes, Mama."

"Why did you not say yes when he asked to see you?" Chided Madame.

"He is so old Mama. You said I did not have to." Replied her daughter, head bowed.

"Yes, but he is rich, do you not see the coffin? He would leave you well provided for daughter."

"Yes, Mama." Her head bowed lower, tears forming.

"Don't 'yes Mama' me daughter, I know you see that no good Marang. He is not good for you. He is only an apprentice. He is not rich like Mr Ashong." Madam scolded as she poked her daughter's side.

"Yes, Mama." Her head bowed further until her chin touched her chest.

"You are a lucky daughter that you are blessed with five older brothers and that you are your father's favourite."

"Yes, Mama." Marisa Jung raised her chin a little, smiling.

As the procession passed Madam Jung, one of the bearer's feet stepped upon a prickle spindle rock and blood poured in thin rivulets like a million little rivers as he lifted his foot. When he put it down again, his leg buckled at the knee and the coffin tottered as he fought for balance. Young Ramana's five-year-old eyes grew wide as the large golden coffin towered over him threatening to fall on him, he wondered if he would die if it hit him or if he would drown in the squishy sea of mud as the coffin pressed and flattened him into the ground; would he become part of the earth unable to speak or move, or would he continue to sink further and further until he reached the centre of the earth, and what would it be like there, would he ever stop or would he continue until came out the other side of the world? In slow motion, the coffin tilted back as the bearer forced his arms up to level with those of the other bearers and he straightened his knee.

The golden coffin passed smoothly now followed by the living coffin. Tradition stated that this coffin be decorated with living insects. Mr Ashong was part of the spider spirit clan, and so this next smooth black coffin had various spiders attached to it, some on their backs and some on their feet. Young Ramana looked at the spider's feet waving and curling as if speaking in a silent physical language, or waving a greeting at all they passed. What if they died before the end of the procession? This would bring black luck to the procession and would cause Mr Ashong great misfortune. He would not be welcomed into the afterlife, his body and bones would disintegrate and shrivel into nothingness and be no more.

The final coffin was made to look like Mr. Ashong's house in every detail, The window openings framed in topaz, the tables and chairs carved of the bahonee wood, and the house filled with jewels of the earth, a fireplace of rubies, plants made of emeralds, mirrors made of diamonds, and piles of pearls were resting couches. As it reached the centre platform pedestal where Mr Ashong sat the coffin tilted to honour him and as it tilted the jewels fell out before him in a rainbow of light, and villagers gasped and fell to their knees to pray that the house of Mr. Ashong would not be destroyed at that moment.

Window on the World

The window was clean, so clear that it seemed as if is was not even there.

The window was her only view of the world, her world existed inside the walls of her home, her fantasy world existed outside the clear glass on the street below.

With a cup of coffee in the morning and tea in the afternoon, she watched as every man, woman and child passed through her life.

She saw the changes in the briskness of their walk, whether they were dressed for sunshine or bundled up against the winter snow. Sometimes the children would be on bikes racing each other down the street or skipping beside their parents.

She saw the love as a woman rested her head against the neck of her lover as they strolled under the canopy of trees that lined the street in spring.

She saw the old couple with the white hair, her arm linked through his as they leaned against each other for support walking slowly through the latter days of their life together.

She knew that years ago she was one of those who first ran down the street chasing her school friends, strolled on the arm of her lover, and then walked alone for the final time to her quiet and solitary flat.

To watch the world from her window, to see other's lives, to not share her life with anyone out there.

She knew out there was love, joy and fun, but it did not outweigh the sadness, the loathing, the loneliness or the fear of venturing past the front door.

She remembered the first time she saw him. He was strolling using the long umbrella like a walking stick, it clicked each time it hit the pavement and silently left when his stride passed it and lifted it with a small swirl and then clicked again as it hit the ground. The curls of his black hair waved against the wind and she could the slash of white against the dark skin when he smiled at a passing girl.

She leaned against the window to watch the last moment of his step and smiled at the beauty of the view.

The next afternoon she moved her chair to the window - her private window on the world.

Reflections of a Snowflake

The streets, grounds, and roofs wear a mantle of white, a light and see-through coating of a myriad of snowflakes.

As I walked back from the store a small part of the mantle cascaded around my shoulders and when I entered my cosy warm home each and every snowflake melted into a part of me, my coat, my scarf, my eyelashes, face, and hair. To ponder and realise that every single snowflake is different each one from the other - just as each one of us is unique yet we encounter and melt and become a part of something else. Then through the mystery and power of nature, the cycle begins again, and a new snowflake is created— again each one unique yet also containing the essence of what it encountered before.

I am unique - yet with each encounter - I melt and become a part of something else - and as the cycle of nature continues so I too am re-created, just like the snowflake.

Becca and Jasmine

"Will you stop with all the death threats - someone somewhere might actually think you're serious! Then what if something did happen? The police would come right here and tote you and your bad ideas right down to jail and then…"

"Okay, okay! Quit lecturing! I'm just venting. Although it is awfully nice to think about him gone forever." Becca leaned back and contemplated her long red nails thinking a spa day was definitely in order. Picking up her mobile phone to rectify the lack of spa time she frowned at the splash of water which showered following the belly flop into the pool and which narrowly missed her newest electronic toy.

Jasmine laughed, "if that breaks it's only the third one this month"

Becca smiled, "nope, the fourth. Didn't tell you about the one that fell in the toilet."

Jasmine rolled her eyes, "I don't even want to know what you were doing with a phone in the toilet.

Becca's response was interrupted

"I go now," announced Helga as she walked past the two sisters. They knew better than to ask. Helga was without a doubt the best baker in town and a wonderful cook. She was also gifted with a domineering personality solely expressed in a matter-of-fact monosyllabic fashion. Almost all who worked for the sisters from the chauffeur to the accountant seemed to become part of the family eventually; all but Helga. For two years she baked at the cafe and cooked at the house but had never shared any part of her personal life. Jasmine and Becca decided long ago not to argue with the irascible personality in case of irritating such a talented baker.

Crossing Helga's path Jason smiled, ignored the grumbling to wink and wave at the receding ball of gloom. He skirted the outside of the oval pool and followed the flagged pathway which was dotted with palm trees, finally seating himself beside Becca.

Jason's eyes crinkled as he smiled widely showing perfect white teeth, in a perfect tanned face. As he slouched comfortably into the chair his shirt opened to show a perfect torso. Jasmine shook her head it was really irritating to think how anyone could look so at ease and perfect on a hot desert summer day, she thought, and if perfect came into view one more time her lunch was definitely going to end up on her plate. She never considered that she was often viewed in the same idyllic and mindful way.

"You're interrupting my…"

"Yes, I am dear one," Jason said interrupting Becca mid-sentence. "But you will be so glad I did."

"Terrible Tony…"

"Don't speak his name!" Becca warned.

"...is no longer a problem." continued Jason without stopping.

"What!" came from the two women in unison.

Jason's smile broadened and he continued.

"His attorney has agreed to the settlement."

"I don't believe it!" Becca exclaimed

"We just made him an offer he couldn't refuse." Jason winked again.

"And will I have any money left?

"Some," replied Jason leaning over the table to open a fresh bottle of white wine.

Becca slumped back, "I am going to need a large glass of that."

"It's not as bad as you think, he will accept a fair cash offer and sign a waiver on your trust."

"He doesn't have any right to that." chimed in Jasmine "That trust was left to us jointly and while Becca married him I certainly did not and if he thinks that he is going to get one dime of that money his brain cells are definitely demented!"

"You're not listening - he doesn't want the money in the trust." Jason hesitated and a small frown appeared.

"What else does he want?" Becca demanded to know.

Jason took his time pouring equal amounts of wine into the three glasses, sighed and plunged forward. "Not much just a few of your paintings and then he'll go away."

Becca's green eyes narrowed as she pulled off her sunglasses as much from emotion as from the bright sunshine.

"Which paintings?"

"Your summer series."

Becca's passion for painting rivalled her mother's but her natural talent far exceed that of her famous mother. Barely twenty-eight-years old Becca could command large sums for her portraits and her seasonal series paintings of which there were only three were valued in the millions.

Part of the value seemed to be generated from the fact that Becca sold only a few of her paintings and the summer series still had to be valued.

"What do you think about killing him now?" Becca asked.

"Well…." mused Jasmine.

Becca looked hopefully at Jasmine who smiled sweetly at her sister.

"What would Dad say?" bringing an end to that conversation.

The time had come Tony had to die, he had ruined her life and she would make him pay. It had taken a long time to get to the place where she could exact the revenge she had been planning. She smiled into the mirror; it was so worth the wait.

"Now when exactly was the last time you saw your husband?

"Soon to be ex-husband," corrected Becca. "Let me see he slithered in here about three months ago trying to worm his way back into the house and we promptly tossed him out."

"Tossed?" ignoring the reptile referral

"Obviously not." Becca retorted. "He is just a bit taller"

Indeed at six foot two inches, Tony had towered over the diminutive Becca who topped five inches at best.

She continued, "Jason escorted him to the door and suggested that if Tony wanted anything at all, to call him and not darken my door again. And why do you want to know? Has he accused me of something?"

The blond young-looking detective viewed the beautiful woman before him and tried to imagine her killing someone and thought with the right provocation she would have absolutely no problem. No more imagining he had to just inform her.

"No, he hasn't accused you of anything and won't. Ever."

Becca raised an eyebrow

"I"m sorry Mrs. Richards, I have to inform you that your husband is dead."

Becca's reaction was immediate disbelief. Tony was a rat on so many levels, but she had loved him once. He couldn't be dead! It was unbelievable to think that he wasn't going to be around to make her life a misery.

Detective Sanders closely watched her reaction, at first the disbelief, then the tears, then the shock and then the questions. You always learned most about the potential suspect by how they reacted to news of a death.

"How? Where?" Jasmine had just appeared in the doorway and entered the room putting her arm around her sister.

Sanders cleared his throat, "He died in your cafe, and we don't have an exact cause of death. There will, of course, be an autopsy and you'll be informed at that time." After a quick assessment, he asked, "and you are his sister-in-law?"

"Yes," Jasmine made a quick judgement of the tall policeman, with his blond curly, hair bronzed skin and light blue eyes he would be more at home on a surfboard rather than visiting families to tell them about the death of a family member.

Becca's tears had dried and curiosity took over. "So, what happened exactly and why do you want to know when I saw him last?

"When a healthy young man is found dead in suspicious circumstances in the business owned by his wife, with whom he has a contentious relationship, we are required to find out the exact events surrounding his death so we can either close the case or ..."

"Open a murder investigation?" Jasmine finished the sentence.

Sanders shifted his appraisal of Becca to the slim sister, as his memory niggled to remind him of where he had seen her before. The transparent sheath did little to hide her tanned slim figure and long legs, and yet again he wished he were somewhere other than this hot desert city, to where he had been banished as a punishment

"Yes." He answered looking her full in the face to gauge her reaction.

Surprising him she smiled although it did not reach the dark blue eyes.

"I"m Jasmine Rhodes, Becca's sister."

Her hand reached out to shake his. He took it and was surprised to find it was cool and dry to the touch despite the fact she had just come in from the pool and summer heat.

"Would you like some water? An iced tea? or an iced coffee?" Jasmine asked as she skilfully guided her sister away from the detective and to the nearby sofa.

"No thank you, ma'am."

Becca disengaged herself from Jasmine and went over to the window, her back facing the room, the only sign of emotion, the clasping and unclasping of her hands.

Damn him she thought, *even in death he was going to cause me problems. It figures, I wanted him to evaporate off the face of the earth and sure enough he's dead. What was that old cliché? Be careful what you wish for?*

Becca's eyes squeezed shut as she tried not to think of his silly lopsided sexy grin, the way he could twist her around his finger just by pouting and putting on the little boy face that she had loved. He was horrible, but she had loved him despite the fights, and the women, until the day he .... she shook her head she did not want to think about it.

She turned back to the room, taking a deep breath. "It's no secret that I wanted him out of my life, but I couldn't do anything to hurt him, I just never wanted to see him again." And with those words, she strolled from the room.

Jasmine's gaze followed her sister and she hesitated. "Will you please let us know exactly what has happened? I'll have our lawyer call you as I'm sure there will be a problem with the cafe and keeping it closed for long." She gazed at him for a moment. "Detective, my sister is quite....passionate, but what she says is true, she couldn't have hurt him, that is if this turns out to be...." and let the possibility hang in the air unspoken.

Leading him to the door she smiled an automatic reaction of farewell and extended her hand again with a simple "goodbye," before closing the door.

Finally, he's dead she thought, as she looked into the mirror and smiled. The first part of the plan has gone according to schedule, now for the second part. Funny the way he had looked at her when he realised what was happening. First, as if she were nothing and then incredulous that not only wasn't she going to help that she was the cause of his demise! She had done it... he was dead... and he had deserved it, after what he had done to her, oh yes. She smiled again into the mirror, the companion who was always there to agree with her and who returned the smile.

"Becca?" Jasmine tapped gently on the bedroom door and entered as soon as she heard her sister's reply.

Becca was sitting dry-eyed staring at the mirror on her dressing table hairbrush in midair, caught between strokes of the long black hair. "Irony doesn't even start to cover this. What happened to him? I know I said I wanted him dead, but I didn't mean it!"

Becca stared as her sister's mirrored reflection. "You think he's been murdered, don't you? But who do you think could have killed him?" She asked.

Jasmine regarded her sister's features, the dark green eyes that were the image of their mother's literally did sparkle like emeralds sometimes, as hokey as that sounded to her own mind. The smooth skin of her forehead was furrowed in puzzlement.

Becca returned her sister's gaze and marvelled at how much Jasmine's expression mirrored their father's whenever there was a little incident. Deep blue eyes changing to sky blue when laughing, her long honey hair swept into the ever-popular ponytail accentuating the long slim neck and shoulders. The beauty and figure that had made her a model at sixteen and only recently retired at twenty-five.

The unspoken look that passed between them communicated, as it always did, the strength of their mutual love which had supported them since the early death of their parents.

"So, where do we start?" Becca broke the silence.

"You really do think that…"

"Yes, I do! And unfortunately, I am probably suspect number one. Yuck, what a mess he is still causing me!" Becca rolled her eyes.

Jasmine squeezed her sister's shoulder. "Okay okay, we might as well start with Jason and see what he can find out."

From the doorway they heard a throat clearing and Becca and Jasmine turned to see Helga.

“Schuldigen," Helga shifted her considerable weight from one foot to the other as if standing on a hot pavement. "Police closed cafe."

Never one to use more words than necessary she stood and waited for a reaction and apparently instructions as to what to do next.

Jasmine stepped forward to ask if Helga had been there, but the baker took two steps back and her eyes widened as if she were about to be interrogated.

Jasmine stopped in her tracks asking, "What happened?"

"Don't know. Wasn't there." Helga kept up the hot pavement dance still waiting for instructions.

Jasmine raised her eyebrows questioningly.

Helga grudgingly used additional words. "Late, had an appointment," and pressed her thick lips together, refusing any further information.

Becca dropped her brush on the dressing table, stood up and turned to give her a sad smile.

"Sorry Helga, we don't know what's going on, so just take a few days off until we find out how best to proceed."

As soon as she saw a frown that distorted Helga's heavy features Becca hurried to add, "paid of course."

"Come on sis, we've got errands to run." Jasmine headed to the door and waited for Helga to head downstairs before following her.

The mirror never lied, it was always her friend, and now it agreed with her expression that all was going according to plan. He was dead, and once the police finally got off the stick and got to work the rest would fall into place. Soon and she would be off on a holiday to celebrate, the red lips formed a happy smile as she contemplated her choices, still she had to be patient, just a few more weeks that was all and it would be finished. I shouldn't have waited this long to kill him was the last thought as she turned from her mirror.

Jason faced the two sisters wondering how to deliver the news. He was young, handsome, a talented and effective lawyer. Still he had always flirted mildly with Becca whose sensual nature appealed to his love of beautiful things and people, but now he had to wear the official lawyer face.

"They're investigating the fact that Tony was poisoned, by digitalis, and they have narrowed the source down to your garden.

"Our garden? How can they know that? And how is that a poison? Digitalis is for your heart." Asked Jasmine.

"Foxglove," answered Becca for once interrupting Jason as the source dawned on her. "It's that purple bell-shaped flower in the back of the garden."

Becca stood up and went to the window. Jasmine crossed her legs and asked how the police could find the direct source.

Jason answered, "not much of it grows here. It needs rich well drained soil, just like the soil in your garden. Also, the garden has quite a large quantity of it and you only need a little. Not to mention that the general public doesn't know what it is and what it can be used for - as a matter of fact, it grows wild in a lot of places."

"It's not just that." Jasmine voiced Becca's thoughts

"Well, think about it, he died in your cafe, with the source of a poison easily available from your garden. For a motive, face it he was working on taking every penny from your sister he could get, so you're both vulnerable. You both have the opportunity, the motive, and well Becca is slightly ahead since she has the means and knowledge about the foxglove."

"What are you going to do?" Becca turned to Jason knowing he would have an idea. "Mitigate everything. Who works in the garden? Who else has access to the cafe? Who else has a motive?"

Jasmine answered the onslaught of questions. "Multiple people work in the garden and the cafe is open to all the students, staff and everyone else on campus, and as for motives let's face it Tony broke rules and women's hearts like it was his profession."

Jason tapped his fingers on the desk. "As long as they can't connect anything directly to you then it should be okay." He hesitated, "Is there anything else you want to tell me?" his gaze shifted from Jasmine to Becca and back.

Without even looking at each other the sisters replied in unison. "No!" then smiled at the harmony in their answer.

As she brushed her hair the mirror mimed the same action. It had brought her the most comfort since he had brought her so much pain! She kept remembering his eyes, those eyes that had lied to so many women, she felt such joy at closing them permanently. The time was passing, too slowly it seemed, but she smiled, feeling safe in knowing that only the reflection knew the truth.

"So, where do we go from here sis? asked Becca as Jasmine finished the phone call.

"Why don't you and I go to the cafe? We haven't been there since the murder and we may get a fresh idea.

It was a ten-minute drive to the cafe on the local college campus and while it was still closed the police had removed all signs of their investigation.

Tony had keeled over in the middle of the lounge area and there was still the mess left from paramedics and police riffling through the entire room. The normally neat and tidy layout had a distinct air of stifling heat and a sickly smell. The sisters surveyed the scene, the bookshelves remained relatively untouched, however, the rest of the large book lined room was a mess with the small tables overturned, lamps askew, a few broken mugs and plates. Since the room revealed nothing Becca headed to the kitchen, noticing that every container had been opened, likely for the samples that the police had taken during their search. Turning to leave she noticed an edge of torn newspaper with a fragment of the picture and it niggled at her memory, it seemed familiar and yet she could not place it. *Where had she seen it before?* She wondered and bending to pick it up she felt her forehead smack into the table as she was hit from behind, and then nothing.

"Becca! Becca!" Jasmine repeated gently lifting her sister's head.

"What the devil happened?" Becca asked as she half opened her eyes, at the same time feeling the back of her head where a lump was growing to match the one already appearing on her forehead.

"Ouch! who hit me?" Asking as she closed her eyes.

"I don't know! I heard a crash and by the time I ran in here the door was shut, and I was more concerned about you than running after some flaming idiotic so-and-so."

"Ya know sis, at a time like this it is okay to swear - even a little." Becca rolled her eyes and then immediately regretted the action.

Jasmine sniffed, "you remember Daddy used to say that those who swear do not have a large enough vocabulary!"

"Only you would remember that at this point in time." Becca commented as she leaned against Jasmine and shakily got to her feet. In slow motion, she propped her elbows on the counter to steady herself and concentrated on trying to remember what happened.

Then it hit her and Becca told Jasmine about the torn newspaper and so for the next few minutes, Jasmine scoured the floor in search of the now missing photo.

"You know sis, I know that I've seen that picture before, I just can't place it, the face was familiar but…"

Becca sat down and closed her eyes to work on remembering the details. This always helped her remember just like sorting the pieces of a puzzle and eventually it would always come together.

"Jasmine, I remember now!" Becca started to get up excited as she recalled the memory, then sat back down again as dizziness threatened.

"It was a torn picture of a young girl Tony dated about two years ago, do you remember that student who killed herself? Remember she was the one who was pregnant, and the article said that she could not face the shame of her family knowing and would not get an abortion. But why would that be here now?"

Both sisters still retained the old style of printed newspapers which were kept in the front lounge area of the café and were always removed once a week. So why would a fragment of a two-year-old article be here in the kitchen? It just didn't make sense.

The mirror reflected the thoughtful gaze, this was going to take some careful handling. Do you believe that the police talked to me several times? The question remained unanswered in the reflection.

Well, just a few more days and all would be resolved. The reflection agreed and smiled in return.

"So how did you figure out it was Helga?" asked Jason as he scooped another mouthful of salsa.

"Becca started me thinking about it," replied Jasmine. "It was that article from two years ago, about the girl who killed herself. I looked up the original article and it said she left a grandmother and that she was of German descent. So, I did a little further searching and found out that the girl was Helga's granddaughter. Something that Helga had failed to mention when she came to work for us. I also discovered that Helga had been a carer nurse in Germany years ago working for a rich client with a heart condition, add to that the fact that she loved gardening, and she had it all motive, means and opportunity. After that, it was just the matter of being able to prove all this, and that's where it got a little sticky.

"Sticky!" exclaimed Becca. "You said the only way to resolve it was a trap, and of course with me as bait.

"Well that is true, but how else we were supposed to get you out of trouble and her into it, I mean she had set you up beautifully, blaming you for not being able to control Tony! As if anyone could have done that!"

Becca sighed, "I suppose, but still it was an awful chance."

"Not with me in the background, looking after you." Added Jason dropping his arm around Becca's shoulders.

Becca snuggled into the embrace as Jasmine rolled her eyes.

"That's it I'm calling Roberto; all this romance is just too much!"

Jasmine smiled thinking of the cute Italian and picked up her mobile phone scrolling to the frequently dialled number.

"Sis, before you do that, maybe you want to have another conversation with that cute blond detective?"

Cherry Blossom Memories

She gazed up into the myriad of pink blossoms that filled the cherry blossom tree. The soft breeze created a gentle cascade of small soft petals, raining sweet wonderful memories. That moonlit night so long ago when he swept her into his arms and touched her lips with his in her very first kiss. A few years later beautiful pale blossoms witnessed when they each promised to love, honour cherish each other and the edible blossoms decorated their wedding cake. She remembered the twins taking their first steps while their pudgy fingers stretched to try and reach the precious blush coloured petals. Memories swirled forward to last week, when their youngest daughter also married under this tree.

Suddenly she felt the familiar gentle embrace and the whisper tickled her ear.

"Strolling down memory lane?"

She turned smiling enfolded in his strong warmth.

"Actually, I'm meandering through the memories of our life, we have shared under the canopy of our lovely cherry blossom tree." She said as she picked an errant petal from his grey hair.

The Coin

She pulled the sleek convertible to a smooth stop. A crossroads, a question, left, or right? The light beams cut through the darkness and inside the small warm space she considered her options. No one was looking for her and she had the open road, and now it posed the question.

So, she slid her hand into her back pocket, the coin was never far away although it had spent time in many hidden places.

She extracted the thin gold coin and as always kissed both sides, heads left and tails right, and with expert ease and flip of her right thumb waited for her future direction to unfold.

She smiled at the result; the coin never failed to surprise her.

She slipped it quickly into her back pocket and with one hand easily turned the wheel.

As the wheels spinned and threw up the gravel and dirt of the road she looked into the rearview mirror, and although the eyes reflected the sadness of leaving, her eyes glistened dark blue with the optimism of the future.

A future that began when the BBQ had ended.

About the Author

Catherine Grace was a journalist, wrote computer tutorials, and worked international corporate events, her creative outlet was always writing stories. This is the first in a series of short stories out for publication. The reason she selected Jasami Publishing Ltd to assist with her first publication is that it aligned with her personal ethos, to give back to the community. Catherine lives in Scotland.

Other Books by this Author

For The Latest Information On

Available Novels

New Releases

&

Coming Soon

Please Visit

JasamiPublishingLtd.com

Printed in Poland
by Amazon Fulfillment
Poland Sp. z o.o., Wrocław

64945757R00058